A HOME FOR LAIKA

AND OTHER TAILS

Thirteen stories featuring mankind's
faithful but sometimes outrageous
four-legged canine companions.

Phillip E. Temples

ISBN: 978-1-945917-66-0

Printed in the United States of America

Cover: Digital illustration by Christopher Reilley
for The Bytesized Studio

Also by Phillip E. Temples:

The Winship Affair
Helltown Chronicles
Machine Feelings and Other Stories
Albey Damned
The Allston Variant
Uncontacted Frontier

"Making other books jealous since 2004"

Big Table Publishing Company
Boston, MA and San Francisco, CA
www.bigtablepublishing.com

Contents

Daggers

Fido's tail normally wags a hundred miles a minute, but right now it's still—limp, in fact. His jaws are slightly ajar and his tongue is firmly ensconced in his mouth.

I know that look. It's rare but I've seen it before. He's shooting daggers at me out of his big, brown angry eyes.

This morning, I mistakenly petted the cat before I petted Fido.

Heart to Heart

"It's a big commitment. I may be misinterpreting, but I think she wants to take it to the next level. That's pretty darn soon, don't you think? After all, we've only been out on three dates.

"I think I like her but I don't know if I love her. Of course, there's the sexual attraction! She's got a killer bod, no question about it. But before I hop into bed with someone again, I just want to make sure. All of my relationships have started out by hopping in the sack. I have sex with a girl and bam! Before I know it, I'm in over my head. Either I find out she's too needy, or she has some really bad vice or annoying habit. Or worse, she's mental! Then there's all the drama of breaking up. God, I hate that part!

"I think that I want to get to know this one a little better, you know? This is definitely new territory for me. This is… this is, like, personal growth, right? Of course, she won't think of it that way. She'll probably interpret it as my being too timid or afraid of making a commitment. She'll drop me before I drop her.

"I guess that wouldn't be the end of the world. It's not as if I haven't been dumped before. There are plenty of fish in the sea, right?

"What would *you* do if you were me? Would you stick to the playbook, or operate outside of your comfort zone?

"Seriously—what would you do?

"Come on. Speak!"

"RUFF, RUFF!"

Streams

Spot whined, barked, even begged his master to take him outside to do his business. He went to the closet, retrieved his leash and laid it at his master's feet to no avail. The master ignored him and instead, continued to watch the reality TV show. Spot could no longer contain his frustration (or bladder). He barked a final warning then he raised his hind leg and let fly a stream of warm urine on the man's foot. Spot's act of desperation elicited a pause on the television remote, followed by a stream of a different type: profanity, the likes of which Spot had never before heard.

Free Will

God perused his/her/its surroundings along with the rest of the universe God created. It was good. It wasn't perfect, but it was good. It seemed like only yesterday that God brought forth a great explosion to start this creation.

God wasn't sure why all of God's creatures believed in a creator who was perfect and all knowing. After all, could they not observe the chaos and strife that surrounded them? God relished the many, many instances where beings treated one another with kindness and compassion. But God could also see numerous examples where things weren't turning out right. It was the price one paid for granting free will, God supposed.

At that moment, God was very unhappy about the wars and slaughter that continued on several far-flung worlds. God had allowed sapience to spring forth in the creations there. Soon after, the beings evolved in intelligence, and developed tools which, unfortunately, were used as weapons of war.

It was always war.

Most wars centered around the need for the creations to define their creator. Why did they feel such a need? Why couldn't they simply be content in not knowing or caring how they came to be? Why destroy others who held different beliefs? Obviously, God was doing something wrong. He/she/it needed to contemplate this and correct it.

God's attention was momentarily diverted when the lady of house came in with a treat in her hand.

"Here, Shango. Come! Mommy has a surprise!"

God stood on hind legs, begged, wagged his/her/its tail furiously and was rewarded with a tasty dog biscuit.

A Home for Laika

On November 3, 1957 a mongrel Soviet space dog named Laika was launched into outer space aboard Sputnik 2. She was the first animal to orbit the earth. The canine was sent up to prove that living beings could survive the launch and provide data on how animals and people would cope with spaceflight. Since the technology to bring back a spacecraft to earth had not yet been developed, Laika was doomed from the beginning. The Soviets claimed that Laika was humanely euthanized before succumbing to oxygen starvation. Still others speculated that she suffered a terrible fate of heat exhaustion. None of these scenarios was true, however.

#

The Glyxonian scout ship orbiting Earth was wrapping up its two-year mission studying our primitive world when its occupants observed the tiny spacecraft achieve orbit. Curious, they rendezvoused with the Sputnik. While they were prohibited from landing on Earth or contacting its inhabitants, there was nothing in the rules about rescuing a Terran stranded in space. They quickly determined that the sole occupant of the spacecraft was in distress.

Laika was, of course, extremely grateful for her rescue. She wagged her tail and licked her rescuers furiously. She was quite willing to accompany the Glyxonians. They, in turn, found Laika to be a delightful and friendly companion. As a parting gift to Laika, the Glyxonians cloned her so that she could be with her own kind. Then they deposited her and her offspring on a virgin planet in a neighboring star system. The planet's earth-like conditions were ideal for Laika and her twenty-three male and female clones. They had no natural predators; plus, there were plenty of smaller animals to chase and eat.

#

Centuries later, when humans land on the Canis 4 system they will be amazed to discover millions of mixed breed husky-terrier dogs—Laikas' offspring—joyously romping about the countryside sniffing each other's butts, humping, and peeing on trees.

Appointed Rounds

Harry had just fastened the leash around Champ's collar and stood up when he felt the tightness in his chest. He pressed the palm of his hand hard against his left breast and caught his breath.

"It's… it's okay, Champ. Nothing…nothing to worry about. It'll pass just like it did last week."

But the pain did not pass. In fact, it intensified. Champ sensed that his master was in distress. He started whimpering.

It was then that Harry glimpsed the tall, dark figure out of the corner of his eye standing near the door. As he turned, Harry saw the unmistakable presence of the Grim Reaper. The mythical character was dressed in black and carried a large scythe. It slowly extended a skeletal finger on its right hand and beckoned. Harry knew that Death had an appointment to collect his soul. Suddenly, the pain in his chest seemed to be the least of his problems.

Champ continued to whimper. A small amount of urine leaked onto the floor from Harry's faithful companion.

"Do you mind?" asked Harry.

The Grim Reaper sighed.

"Well…okay. Just be quick about it. I'm on a tight schedule."

Harry nodded his thanks as he pressed past Death out the door with Champ in tow.

Intervention

"I'd like to sniff her butt," remarked the young French bulldog named Pierre to his friend, Max. The object of Pierre's attention was a tall, elegant standard poodle who came prancing into the training room with her owner. Max was a four-year-old longhaired, purebred Irish setter with impeccable grooming. He possessed an angular, wiry frame, and a long head with a coat straighter than that of the English breeds. His fur was a deep orange-red color. The bitches found him quite attractive.

Max was deeply embarrassed by Pierre's comment. "Mind your manners, if you even have any. We're in mixed company here."

Pierre started to giggle, but the giggling soon turned into a violent sneezing fit. After it was over, mucus drooled from his snout. He shook his head vigorously to and fro, in an effort to clear away the snot. Some of it flew into Max's face.

"Aw! Disgusting!" cried Max.

"Damned sinuses," said Pierre.

"I don't know why I hang out with you."

Pierre grinned. "Could it have something to do with my loveable personality?"

"Yes, I suppose it would *have* to be your personality, given the fact that your face looks like it was run over by a garbage truck."

"I'll pretend that I didn't hear that. You can say what you will about this mug, my furry friend, but I bet you a week's supply of dog biscuits that I get laid more than you."

Max sighed. "No contest. Hey, perhaps I should refer my friend, Theodore, to you for dating advice. His idea of good sex is humping his master's leg."

"That's just plain wrong," said Pierre.

Just then, a woman with the Chihuahua named Sissy stepped between them, headed for the middle of the room. Sissy stopped long enough to shoot both of them dirty looks as she trotted by. Her owner jerked on Sissy's collar and urged her forward. The trainer was demonstrating today the fine art of hand-signal commands to heel and to fetch.

"So, uh, Max, who's the cat I've seen you hanging out with?" Pierre asked.

Max hesitated for a second.

"That's Frita. She's—she's a friend."

The trainer was snapping his fingers, pointing at Sissy. Sissy looked confused and frustrated; she was unsure what was expected of her. Her owner scowled at Sissy.

"Dumb bitch!" exclaimed Pierre. "Doesn't Sissy know to park her ass on the floor when the guy points like that?"

The Chihuahua pretended to not hear Pierre.

"Shhsh! That was rude!" exclaimed Max.

Pierre ignored him and continued with his earlier line of questioning.

"Frita, huh? You're on a first name basis with a cat, now? And exactly what, pray tell, do you see in this cat, anyways? If you ask me, you should be hangin' out more with your own kind, not some feline. I hate to tell you this, Max, but there's gossip—"

"I don't care what the other dogs are saying, Pierre. My personal life is *my* business. Frita is polite, well mannered, and highly intelligent. We talk a lot, and we have fun, and we enjoy each other's company which is more than I can say for yours right now."

Pierre eyed his friend suspiciously. "Don't tell me you're…you're not falling for this pussy, are you?"

"What if I am?" shot back Max.

"But, it ain't *natural*, Max! In fact, it's just plain queer if you ask me."

"No one's asking you."

"Max, how the heck would you…you know, put *your* thing in *her* thing? They wouldn't even fit."

"There's more to relationships than sex, Pierre."

"I suppose her idea of foreplay would be to slap you across the face with her claws fully extended until she draws blood, and then purr sweet nothings in your ear."

At that instant, it was Max's and his owner's turn to enter the circle. She tugged at Max's collar and urged him forward.

Thank god, saved by the bell.

"Pervert!" barked Pierre at Max, as Max was led away. Max craned his head back at Pierre. He shot Pierre an evil glare.

Several of the other dogs heard the comment and were looking inquisitively at Pierre. A couple of them asked what the altercation was about. It wasn't long before the entire group received an ear full from Pierre about their "queer" friend, and his relationship with the cat, Frita. The terrier was the first to suggest it.

"I think it's time for an intervention. We have to sit Max down and make him see that he's headed down a very dangerous path."

"Yeah," barked the Dalmatian. That's some sick stuff. Max isn't sniffin' straight. That cat's got him brainwashed. Maybe's she's been slippin' him catnip."

"Can dogs even get *high* on catnip?" asked the Rottweiler.

"Who knows?" replied Pierre. "But I know this: Max has been off his feed for a few weeks now. This explains it."

"I say we confront him at the next session," exclaimed the Terrier. "All in favor, bark 'aye.'"

\#

The following week, Max arrived with his owner in tow. He was careful to lead her at just the appropriate walking pace; it was a well-known fact that humans were hampered in their walking abilities since they possessed only two feet. Thus, certain accommodations had to be made.

As the two entered to room, Max looked around at all the other canines who were already present. The owners stood clumped in groups, prattling on with each other about gods-knows-what. But the canines stood silently. They avoided looking Max in the eye—all except Pierre. Pierre was glaring at Max.

Max was beginning to feel very uncomfortable. *What's going on? What did that son of a bitch tell them?* Just then, he caught a flash of fur out of the corner of his eye. *There—outside the window. It's Frita! What is she doing here?*

The cat paced on the windowsill, peering in, her tail jerking to and fro. Max hoped the others hadn't seen her.

"Max?" Cal, the old Terrier, addressed him.

"I think I speak for everyone here when I say—"

Just then, the Rottweiler spotted Frita in the window. He uttered an incredibly loud growl that immediately alerted the others. They, in turn, proceeded to howl, bay, yelp, and woof in a cacophony of alarm and displeasure at the sight of the feline interloper.

The dashhound was the first to spot it. Max's owner had not securely fastened the door upon entering the room earlier. It was ajar slightly. The hound leapt for the door; she got one foot between the door and the door jam and succeeded in prying it open. That was all it took.

The others slipped from their owners' grasps; some were off leash, while others dragged their leashes behind them as they hurried at a breakneck pace toward the screen door on the back porch. The humans were completely taken by surprise. In fact, no one even reacted at first.

"Come back here!" they finally cried.

"Don't hurt her!" barked Max.

But his plea fell on deaf ears. Once outside, the excited pack rounded the corner of the house and zeroed in on the startled, shorthaired domestic cat. Frita leapt from the windowsill and lit off for home as though she was being pursued by a thousand demons. The pack stayed on her trail for only a moment. Of course, they realized it would be a fruitless chase. Nevertheless it felt glorious! The chase was more fun than staying inside and performing stupid obedience tricks for the humans.

Max looked around the room. All the owners were outside retrieving their canines. He and Pierre were the only one's present.

"I thought you were my friend," said Max. The bitterness in his bark was palpable.

"Hey, buddy, 'who's your buddy?' Come on pal. Lighten up! The group called for this intervention because we care for you. Besides, you'll thank me someday."

Pierre walked over to Max. He was moved by the sadness he saw in Max's eyes. In that moment, Pierre realized he had genuinely hurt Max. He was overcome with shame for betraying best friend. Pierre wanted to apologize, but words failed him.

"I…I…" Pierre sighed. "Sorry, Max."

Pierre put his head down between his legs and bowed to Max in a sign of submissiveness. Max, however, was still fuming from the whole ordeal.

As the dogs began filing back in to the room, they witnessed an unbelievable sight: the normally well-mannered, mature Max had his hind leg hiked in the air, and was aiming his pee right for Pierre's head!

"You'll *thank* me someday," he growled. "Speciesist!"

Obedience School

The obedience school trainer was beginning to lose his patience with one particular pupil—Philip, "Lip" for short. The spirited English Bulldog was being especially stubborn on that day of all days—graduation. All of the dog owners were present to see their prize companions respond to commands to "drop it," "stay," "sit," and "lie down."

Each dog performed to perfection until it was Lip's turn. The trainer was a firm believer in positive reinforcement, but in this particular situation he realized that negative reinforcement might be called for. The trainer jerked hard on Lip's leash and repeated the command harshly.

"Lie down!"

Lip looked up at the trainer defiantly, sporting a wrinkled, pudgy face that only a mother could love. "NO!" said the dog.

There were gasps from all of the humans in the large room.

"Wh—what did you say?"

Lip looked up at him, with drool dripping out of the side of his left jowl. "No. *Sir*! There. Is that respectful enough?"

A Beautiful, Symbiotic Relationship

I wonder if things would have turned out differently had our canine friends not become so friendly with early *Homo sapiens* watching with envy as the the cavemen roasted their fresh kill over an open fire. Although drawn in by the delicious smell of food, the wary canines kept their distance. Surely, they must have wondered how this weak pack of humans—disorganized and unable to run fast or bite hard—could have harnessed the power of pain-light.

It probably started something like this: a solitary canine, lost or even ostracized by her pack, ventured near the camp. We'll call her "Beatrice" but they probably called her "Uggnah." Hunger eventually overcame Beatrice's fear of the hurtlight. She crept close. One of the younger *Homo sapiens* saw the dog and took pity on her. Beatrice acted submissively; perhaps she even whimpered a little bit to play it up. When the adults weren't looking, the boy threw a morsel of food in Beatrice's direction. Beatrice lapped it up quickly. Little by little, the dog overcame her fear, venturing closer to the humans and their fire and accepting more morsels. At one point she drew so close that the boy could almost reach out and touch her. The adults noticed this behavior; a few even encouraged it. Beatrice grew more relaxed in their presence, and they in hers.

Beatrice started following them out on their hunts. She was a smart creature. She figured out how to help the humans hunt by circling their prey and startling them so that they would run directly into a trap where the humans lay in wait with spears and rocks in hand. Other troops of humans began to notice this behavior. They, too, befriended solitary Ugg-nahs and domesticated them. It was the beginning of a beautiful, symbiotic relationship.

But try explaining *that* to the poor, shivering Chihuahua of today—dragged about on the freezing streets of South Boston and dressed from head to toe in a silly green costume for St. Patrick's Day.

Conspiracy

"Raff, we gotta talk." The man entered the study. It was unoccupied except for the presence of the family dog, Raphael. He looked at the dog with disgust. "Would you stop licking your balls for a minute and listen!"

The dog paused and looked up at the man, his hind leg still pointing up at the ceiling. "Okay, okay! You don't have to be so grumpy. I'm listening. What's on your mind?"

The man sighed. "You have to stop terrorizing Fluffy. Doris is getting really upset."

"Oh, the cat. What is Fluffy alleging I did now? You realize, if I so much as look askance at that mangy ball of fur, she gets offended and starts spreading innuendos and outright lies."

"So, you *didn't* chase her out into the street yesterday?"

"She…there was…Look, I was barking at a car driving by. How was *I* to know that Fluffy was in the yard, too? She might have…misinterpreted my actions and thought that I was barking at her. As you know, cats aren't terribly smart. At any rate, no harm, no foul. The car got away but Fluffy wasn't hurt."

"I heard that it was a close call. Doris says Fluffy ran right in front of the car as it passed. And that's not the only incident. You were heard growling at Fluffy when Doris fed the two of you on Saturday."

Raphael shook his head vigorously. His dog tags made a loud clanging sound as they rattled against each other. "She started it! Do you see this scratch on my nose? I was merely expressing my displeasure over constantly finding cat fur in my dog bowl. It's bad enough that the fur permeates the air but now I have to eat it, too?"

"Yeah, well, you've got a point there," said the man. "My allergies have been kicking up something fierce of late. I'm sure that it's not you."

"Well, there you have it, then," said the dog. "That cat's got to go."

The man made a grimace at the dog's absurd suggestion.

"Look, hear me out. It's not as ridiculous as it sounds. I have a plan. Wanna hear it, human?"

Hurry Up and Find God

It was a fabulous day for man and his beast to take a walk in the nearby park. The dog was lost in thought as he trotted along. He didn't even stop to take in the smells of the myriad canines and other creatures that had previously peed along the path.

Should not man and beast always be mindful of finding God in nature, both in sight and smell? After all, Henry David Thoreau's metaphysical convictions compelled him to defend nature's intrinsic values in a way that aligns him philosophically "far removed from Emerson and other transcendentalists." At least, that's what Cafaro wrote.

Indeed, Thoreau would argue that the person who is unmoved by the beauty of things is the one with a flawed perception of reality, since it is the unenlightened observer who is less well aware of the world as it is.

Meanwhile, the man walked impatiently behind the dog. His thoughts were decidedly less metaphysical: *Would you hurry up and do your business, ya' dumb dog?*

Record Breaker

Tyler Lawson and Billy Hajo came across the giant Burmese Python in an Ochopee, Florida subdivision lot and realized it was close to record-breaking size.

"It's long enough, Billy, but it looks to be a few pounds shy of the one they caught over in Sylvan Shores last month."

All the while, a standard poodle barked incessantly at the duo and the snake from behind a neighbor's fence. Tyler and Billy came up with the solution to attaining a record-breaker almost simultaneously. As an added bonus, there was no more racket.

Mixed Breed

Vern and Fran sat under a shady tree next to their rig in the Yogi Bear RV Camp & Resort in New Hampshire's White Mountains and Lakes Region. It was a busy fall weekend; there were few vacancies to be had. That day, the couple had perused all the other rigs with license plates spanning nearly twenty states. The most prominent state was their newly adopted "home" of South Dakota. Vern and Fran, who were life-long Illinois residents, had switched just last year. South Dakota was known for its lack of state tax and easy mail forwarding, along with a host of other pluses that lured retirees to switch their residency.

Recently retired, the couple had sold their ranch home and bought a 42-foot Newman Mountain Aire diesel pusher. It sported a Jeep tow vehicle, four slides, and a motorcycle lift. It even had a stacked washer-dryer so they wouldn't be at the mercy of the expensive camp Laundromats. Their rig was the envy of many at the RV campgrounds in which they stayed.

"Yep Fran, I'd say we take the prize this weekend. Haven't seen anything bigger 'n us so far," commented Vern. The two had just returned from walking their two small dogs, a young Chihuahua named Elizabeth, and an aging pug named Livingston-Maxwell.

"C'mon, Max, up you go!" urged Vern. The pug snorted intensely, then it sneezed. After Vernon encouraged him a few more times, Maxwell leapt with all his might, and almost succeeded in making it up one of Vernon's legs and onto his lap. Vernon grabbed onto the aging mutt and hauled him up the rest of the way.

"Good boy, good boy!" Vern exclaimed. Maxwell reached up and licked Vern's face in a show of adoration.

Fran brought out a pitcher of tea and set it down on a foldout table. They didn't even have time for a sip before a glint of light caught their attention. A new rig was pulling into the camp. They stared at it in disbelief.

It was an odd-looking affair: long, silver in color, and sporting aerodynamic features. Vern reckoned it to be least a 50-footer, and then some. It was eerily silent. There were strange do-hickeys spaced at regular intervals along its base; he had no idea as to their purpose. The windows looked more like portals and the front windshield resembled that of an airplane's. There were no visible manufacturer's markings to be seen. The rig's wheel wells were completely covered, giving it the appearance of floating along the road. It proceeded slowly for another hundred feet then it pulled effortlessly into the park's last remaining, empty space.

The couple continued to stare. "Would you look at that, Vernon!"

#

Eventually, curiosity got the better of the two and after supper, Vern and Fran decided to take a walk down the road to see the strange rig up close. They brought Livingston-Maxwell and Elizabeth with them. As they approached the silver monstrosity, Vern and Fran could see its two occupants enjoying a meal outside. The man and woman appeared to be in their early twenties. Both wore short-cropped, blonde hair. They had a small animal at their side; at first, Vern mistook it for a hairless cat but upon closer examination, it appeared to be some sort of Chihuahua-mixed breed. It was excited; upon seeing Vern and Fran's canines, the critter emitted a high-pitched yelp and proceeded to jump several feet into the air. In response, Elizabeth also pranced around excitedly. The woman shot her animal a stern stare; it immediately sat on the ground and looked at her obediently. The old dog, Maxwell, simply stood there and drooled.

"Hello!" the man called to Vern and Fran. "Would you like to sit and talk?"

"Thanks. Don't mind if we do. I'm Vernon Stockwell. This is my wife, Fran."

The two newcomers introduced themselves as John and Jane Doe. They were from Las Vegas and had recently taken up the RV lifestyle. The Does offered Vern and Fran some lemonade.

"I hope you don't mind me sayin' this, John, but you two look awfully young to be retired," chuckled Fran.

John smiled. "No, we're still…working. We're just taking a break from things for a while. You see, Jane and I, um, work for the government at an engineering facility. Occasionally they let us out for good behavior." Jane laughed at his joke.

"I see. They must treat you pretty well out there."

Vern looked again at the silver bullet.

"This is quite a rig you got here, John. I was tellin' Fran, I ain't never seen one quite like it. Who makes it, anyways?"

John paused to take a sip of lemonade.

"It's a custom job, Vern. You see I, ah…I like to design things in my spare time. Jane and I had this vacation planned for some time, and I had the folks in the machine shop at work construct this recreational vehicle to my specifications. I guarantee you, you won't find another one like it anywhere in the…on the planet."

"Can I take a look at the controls?"

Jane shot John a peculiar look. Fran thought that she looked embarrassed, perhaps even frightened.

"Ah, maybe tomorrow?" Jane asked. "It's been a long drive and things are pretty messy right now."

"Oh sure, no problem, folks," Vern replied. "We understand. Livin' on the road, things can get pretty disorganized. Especially when your pets are running all over and…"

Just then, the couples heard a howl coming from behind the Doe's rig. It sounded like something between fear and ecstasy. The Chihuahua, Elizabeth, came running from around the corner, followed in hot pursuit by John and Jane's dog. The animal caught up with Elizabeth; he mounted the small dog and proceeded to hump it frantically. Elizabeth howled some more.

"Zyforg!" shouted Jane. She pointed at the ground next to her chair.

The dog immediately stopped its mating, and trotted over and sat under the chair. Vern couldn't help but notice the dog's enormous, erect penis.

"I'm so sorry!" said Jane. "When our animal gets 'excited' it can sometimes misbehave around other animals. I hope your dog wasn't traumatized."

Vern and Fran exchanged glances. Fran said, meekly, "No harm done. She's been spayed." Vern added, "It's a doggie's nature, I suppose."

The two chatted about their respective pets. Vern and Fran told them that their pug, Livingston-Maxwell, had been in the family for almost ten years. They had picked up Elizabeth at a pound in Santa Fe last year to keep Maxwell company. Max didn't cotton to the younger pup at first, but the two were now best of friends.

"What did you call your dog? Ziferg?"

"Zyforg," said Jane. "It's a rather unusual name. You see, John is an amateur astronomer. He named the animal after a distant planet that orbits Sirius."

Huh, that's odd, Vern thought. *Didn't they give all those exoplanets names like Keplar 69-c and such?*

"I see. And what kind of breed is your Zyforg? Looks like he's got a little bit of Chihuahua in 'em. And, no offense—he looks like he's got more 'cat' in 'em than dog."

"He's a special breed, very unique. It's called—"

"Jane interrupted. "It's called 'Azawskrozi.'"

"Yes," replied John. "Azawskrozi. You see, we picked him up on a trip to…the Galápagos Islands several few years ago. There are all sorts of animal breeds living on the island that can be found nowhere else. Are you familiar with Darwin's theory of evolution?"

John and Jane proceeded to lecture to them about Darwin's early work on the island and all of the mysterious creatures he had encountered. Vern and Fran were quite impressed by the lesson but also, a bit overwhelmed. It seemed that the young couple possessed considerable knowledge about a great many things. But there was one thing that Vern and Fran knew a lot about, too—dogs and dog breeding.

"Now, this critter of yours," began Vern, "Zyforg. You say he's a pure breed 'Azawskrozi'? Have you ever thought about entering him in competition?"

John and Jane exchanged surprised looks.

"No. Please tell us more!"

For the next fifteen minutes, Fran and Vern discussed their favorite pastime: being on the dog show circuit. They had been quite active until just a few years ago, up until they sold their home and hit the road. The couple had placed in numerous small breed competitions throughout the south and the east coast. They described to John and Jane how thrilling it was to watch a judge come up and handle their animal, observe its good grooming, and how obedient and conforming it was when put to the test.

"You say these contests are held all over the United States?" asked Jane.

"Oh sure," replied Fran. We used to load up our dogs in the van and travel to a show nearly every weekend. Why, this weekend you'll probably find...well, let's see..."

Fran pulled out her smartphone and Googled a schedule of upcoming shows.

"Here," she said, gesturing at the phone. "Tomorrow morning, there's a big one sponsored by the American Kennel Club in Richmond, Virginia."

Jane looked at the phone and then she glanced anxiously at John. "We *have* to do this, John. This is exciting!"

"Whoa, folks! There's a lot of training and preparation involved," said Vern. "You have to start with the basics. Now, this here show in Richmond—it's pretty advanced. And besides, Richmond is a far piece from New Hampshire. Even driving nonstop, it would take you the better part of thirteen to fourteen hours to get there—unless, of course, that rig of yours can sprout wings."

Vern laughed at his own joke. At first, John and Jane looked blankly at one another. A second later, they, too, laughed.

"Of course, you're absolutely right, Vern," replied Jane. "I guess I let myself get carried away there for a moment. Virginia *is* awfully far away and besides, we would need to 'train' our animal to be more obedient, wouldn't we?" She smiled at John.

"Yes, that's a lot of driving," replied John. "I don't think we're up for that challenge. In fact, I am actually feeling a bit tired. So if you folks will excuse us, I think we will tidy up a bit, and turn in early. But thanks so much for telling us about the dog shows."

\#

Vern awoke with a start. At first, he was confused. Their bedroom was bathed in an intense light coming from outside the rig. It penetrated their custom, room-darkening blinds.

What the—!

He looked over at the clock on the dresser; it displayed 3:27 AM.

"Wake up, dear! Something's going on."

Fran rolled over and opened her eyes; she, too, was instantly awake. They both rushed out of bed and nearly tripped over one another as they made their way to the outer door.

"Would you look at that?!"

Fran, Vern, and dozens of other residents of the Yogi Bear RV Camp stood outside and shielded their eyes, as they looked skyward at the brilliant flying object hovering almost directly above them. The thing hung in mid-air for another twenty seconds, then it blasted off in a southerly direction at an incredible speed. The entire time, it was completely silent. After only a few seconds had elapsed, it had shrunk to a small pinpoint of light.

Moments later, after his vision had returned to normal, Vern started a conversation with their neighbors in the RV next door. The husband and wife, who were from Oregon, were also baffled by the unidentified flying object. Johnny, a retired Marine "Gunny" boasted that it was one of those stealth helicopters, "like the one they used to take out Osama bin Laden."

"Well," Johnny's wife remarked, "It sure did take off like a 'bat out of hell.'"

It was then that Vern happened to look down the road and realized the Doe's rig was missing.

#

The following morning, Fran and Vern rose from their slumber. Fran was still rubbing the sleep from her eyes and wondering if they had imagined the whole episode with the UFO, when she heard peeping sounds coming from the living room. Fran put on her slippers and walked the short distance from the bedroom to the couch. There she saw another incredible sight.

"Vernon…you better come in here. You're never going to believe this!"

Vern joined Fran. Both peered behind the couch at the source of the sound. Their two-year-old spayed Chihuahua, Elizabeth, was nursing a litter of six newborn Azawskrozi-Chihuahua puppies.

About the Author

Phillip E. Temples resides in Watertown, Massachusetts. He's published four mystery-thriller novels, a novella, and a short story anthology in addition to over 150 short stories. Phil is a member of New England Science Fiction Association, the Mystery Writers of America and the Bagel Bards. You can learn more about him at Temples.com.

www.ingramcontent.com/pod-product-compliance
Lightning Source LLC
Chambersburg PA
CBHW060356180626
46817CB00008B/3040